For my mom, Carol F. Holmes,
and for my grand-auntie, Delia Shuter.

NIC

For Cameron, Jeffrey and Carol.

KL

Shin-chi's Canoe

Nicola I. Campbell

PICTURES BY
Kim LaFave

GROUNDWOOD BOOKS   HOUSE OF ANANSI PRESS   TORONTO   BERKELEY

Acknowledgments to our elders and survivors of Indian Residential School. Kᵂukᵂscemxᵂ

Text copyright © 2008 by Nicola I. Campbell
Illustrations copyright © 2008 by Kim LaFave
Published in Canada and the USA in 2008 by Groundwood Books
Second printing 2009

Groundwood Books / House of Anansi Press
110 Spadina Avenue, Suite 801, Toronto, Ontario M5V 2K4
or c/o Publishers Group West
1700 Fourth Street, Berkeley, CA 94710

We acknowledge for their financial support of our publishing program
the Canada Council for the Arts, the Government of Canada through the Book Publishing
Industry Development Program (BPIDP) and the Ontario Arts Council.

ONTARIO ARTS COUNCIL
CONSEIL DES ARTS DE L'ONTARIO

Library and Archives Canada Cataloguing in Publication
Campbell, Nicola I.
Shin-chi's canoe / Nicola I. Campbell ; illustrations by Kim LaFave.
ISBN-13: 978-0-88899-857-6
ISBN-10: 0-88899-857-0
I. LaFave, Kim II. Title.
PS8605.A5475S556 2008   jC813'.6   C2008-900583-X

Design by Michael Solomon

A NOTE ON THE ART
Sketches were redrawn in Prisma pencil on 140-lb. cold-pressed watercolor paper.
These final drawings were then scanned and the resulting digital images colored on the computer
using Corel Painter and Photoshop.

Printed and bound in China

Imagine North America without buildings, cars and electricity. You can only eat what you gather, hunt or catch. You get fresh water from the creek. Your home was built using trees and animal hides, or it is underground. Your people live by their own rules and take care of their families and communities. As a child, you are surrounded by the love of your family and community.

When Europeans came to the Americas they believed Native people were uncivilized. They pushed them off their traditional lands and onto reserves, or reservations. In the late 1800s governments decided to colonize Native people, forcing them to adapt to the European way of life. In both Canada and the US (as well as in Australia and New Zealand), laws were passed forcing Native children to be educated in church-run boarding schools. The purpose of these schools was to sever all ties the children had to their families, cultures and traditional territories.

While attending these schools the children learned European culture, religion and language. They were given European names. They learned how to grow a garden, run a farm and do carpentry. The children weren't allowed to talk to their parents or their siblings. They weren't allowed to speak their traditional language or practice their traditional way of life. Sometimes the children weren't allowed to return home for many years; sometimes they never returned. Although some children had good experiences, many did not.

There were approximately 130 Indian residential schools in Canada, and about 80,000 people living today attended those schools. Although most closed in the 1970s, the last government-operated residential school in Canada did not close until 1996. More than 100,000 Native American children were forced to attend similar schools in the United States.

In order to make up for the devastating experiences of being sent to these schools, governments around the world have tried to make amends in various ways – either through financial compensation, such as the Common Experience Payment offered to living survivors by the Canadian government, or through formal apology. However nothing can make up for the tremendous loss of language, culture and family.

Steadfast resistance, determination, courage, healing, strength of spirit and an overwhelming love for our children and culture are the tremendous forces that have empowered indigenous peoples around the world to overcome the profound impact that this part of history has had on them.

Nicola I. Campbell

The morning sun was shining so bright,
Shi-shi-etko had to squint.
She was on her way back to
Indian residential school
and this year she wasn't alone.
Shin-chi, her younger brother, was coming, too.

Yayah, Mom, Dad, baby Shultetko,
Shin-chi and Shi-shi-etko
were sitting together on the porch,
waiting for the cattle truck that would soon pick them up.

"Dad, it'll be summertime when we come home.
Can you please build us a dugout canoe of our own?" Shin-chi said.

"My children, don't you like paddling with me anymore?"
said their dad as he pulled them close.

"We love paddling with you!" Shi-shi-etko said.

"But we're getting way too old and
I want to learn to paddle all alone,"
said Shin-chi, who was six years old.

Last year, on her first day at Indian residential school,
Shi-shi-etko had been punished because
she could not understand the English words.
Then they cut her long braids and threw
     them away
and washed her head with kerosene.
And so that morning, before the
     sun rose,
Shi-shi-etko asked,
     "Yayah, can you cut
     our hair today?"

Afterwards, Shin-chi, Shi-shi-etko and Yayah
went up the mountain to put their braids away.

When the cattle truck arrived,
their dad tucked a tiny canoe into Shi-shi-etko's hand.
"My children," their mom said, with tears in her eyes.
"If we could, we would keep you here at home.
We would never, ever let you go, but it's the laws
that force us to send you away to residential school."

Yayah squeezed them so tight
    they could hardly breathe.
"We'll be waiting for you to come home," she said.
Then Shin-chi and Shi-shi-etko climbed into the back
    of the cattle truck
with all the children from their Indian reservation.

Dust came in waves,
getting in their eyes and in their noses,
until they could hardly breathe.
It followed the truck like a snake
all along the valley.

"My Shin-chi, we will not see our family
until the sockeye salmon return.
These are the things you must always remember,"
Shi-shi-etko said, gesturing to the trees, mountains and river below.

"At night, when you go to sleep,
remember the tug of the fish
when you and Dad pulled the nets in
and we made smoked and wind-dried salmon."

Shin-chi could not help himself.
He looked at everything —
the mountain with the trail that led to the caves, the deer in the field by their house.
He memorized every fishing spot, the place where he caught the great big frog,
the grasshoppers, the crickets and the slugs,
until the rattle bump of the cattle truck rocked him to sleep.

Shin-chi was dreaming when he heard Shi-shi-etko say,
"It's time to wake up now, my Shin-chi."
When he opened his eyes it was dusk, and
all he could see was the dark silhouette of the church steeple.

"Remember, my English name is Mary.
Your English name is David. And don't forget,
we aren't allowed to talk to each other until next June."

Shi-shi-etko gave him the tiny canoe that their father had made.
"This, my Shin-chi, is for you.
No matter where you go, no matter what you do,
be careful to keep it hidden."

When they got off the truck the priests and sisters said,
"Juniors and intermediates, stand single file in
    separate lines.
Boys stand here, girls stand over there."
Then single file they marched inside.

That night, in the junior girls' wing,
Shi-shi-etko wondered if her Shin-chi was okay.
He was used to sleeping near his sisters.
He had never slept alone.

Down the hall, in the junior boys' wing,
Shin-chi lay in bed wide awake.
He held his tiny canoe safely in his hands.
The sweet scent of cedar smelled just like his dad.

"Dad said the spring salmon come up the river first,
then the sockeye come in the summertime.
That's when we can go home again."
Finally, he drifted off to sleep.

They went to mass once each day.
That's where they learned how to pray.
For half a day they worked,
the other half they went to school.

The girls did the cooking, cleaning, knit mittens and scarves,
and they laundered and sewed everyone's clothes.
The boys learned how to farm, do carpentry and blacksmithing.
And three times a day all the children went outside to play
in wind, rain, hail or snow.

In the dinner hall the boys and girls sat on opposite sides of the room,
brothers and sisters not allowed to talk to one another.
They made up sign language to say, "Hi," or "I miss you."

For breakfast the children ate porridge and burnt toast.
Through the doors they could see their teachers carrying
steaming plates of bacon, eggs and potatoes from the farm.

For lunch they ate thin soup,
and dinner was hard buns with stew.
For dinner the teachers had meat,
vegetables and corn.
The children were never given
enough food.

When autumn was over and winter arrived,
the days were short and the weather cold.
Shin-chi was lonely and he was hungry.
He missed his mom, his dad and Yayah.
He missed Shi-shi-etko
and baby Shul-tetko, too.

He snuck out the back door and ran
to the river nearby his school.
He stood there with his
tiny dugout canoe.

Shin-chi could not help himself.
He looked at everything.
He listened to each crystal snowflake
that danced down from the sky and fell on his face.
He breathed the cool breath of winter,
until the land was covered in a blanket of fresh snow.

Finally, when eagle song echoed through the valley,
traveling just beyond reach,
he sang his grandfather's prayer song and
his voice echoed from mountain peak to mountain peak.

Shin-chi placed his canoe in the river,
knowing that the current
would carry it safely home.

Then Shin-chi made a friend.
His English name was John.
Little mischief times two,
they learned how to steal food.
In the orchards they found apples,
in the root cellar carrots and potatoes.
To their delight one day they discovered
    preserved cherries
only to realize they had black olives instead.

Early one morning, when spring had finally set in,
Shi-shi-etko snuck down to the river.
To her surprise she heard her grandfather's song.
Her Shin-chi was already there with his fishing line.

"I'm checking to see if the sockeye salmon are here,"
he said, in deep concentration.
"Not yet, my Shin-chi, but they will come."

When the sockeye finally swam up the river,
the dust rose around the cattle truck
like a great big butterfly
that followed them all the way home.

Shin-chi could hardly wait.
"Shi-shi-etko," he asked over and over again,
"how much longer till we get home?"

"Little mischief, you, we'll get there soon,"
Shi-shi-etko said, with sparkles in her eyes.

When the cattle truck arrived at last,
their mother and Yayah ran to greet them.
"Oh, my grandchildren, we missed you!"
Yayah said, squeezing them tight.

"Your dad is in the woodshed,"
said their mom as she hugged them, too.
This time she had tears of happiness in her eyes.

Shi-shi-etko and Shin-chi ran as fast as they could
all the way to the woodshed.
There they found their dad carving them
their very own dugout canoe.